Two eggs, please.

For the two new babies in town, Grace and McGhee
—S. W.

To John and Marie Simmons, a couple of good eggs.
Thanks to the Cheyenne Diner and to Lupeta,
who showed me how to hold eight plates at once
—B. L.

Two eggs, please.

written by
SARAH WEEKS

illustrated by
BETSY LEWIN

Aladdin Paperbacks • New York London Toronto Sydney

Two eggs, please.
Fried.
Side of bacon,
hash browns,
corn muffin, sausage,
OJ, and a lightly toasted
sesame-seed bagel
with cream cheese—
no butter.

"Two sunny-side up!"

"Two over easy!"

"Two scrambled!"

"Two soft-boiled!
Two hard-boiled!"

"Two on a roll!"

"Two fried!"

"Two poached!
Two raw!"

Different.

The same.

"Two eggs coming up!"

Different . . .

but the same.

ALADDIN PAPERBACKS

An imprint of Simon & Schuster Children's Publishing Division

1230 Avenue of the Americas, New York, NY 10020

Text copyright © 2003 by Sarah Weeks

Illustrations copyright © 2003 by Betsy Lewin

ALADDIN PAPERBACKS and colophon are
trademarks of Simon & Schuster, Inc.

Also available in an Atheneum Books for Young Readers hardcover edition.

Designed by Ann Bobco.

The text of this book was set in Base Mono, Berliner Grotesk, Blockhead,
Bodega Serif, Cafeteria, Clicker, Comic Sans, and Meta.

The illustrations for this book were rendered in watercolor and ink.

Manufactured in China

First Aladdin Paperbacks edition January 2007

2 4 6 8 10 9 7 5 3 1

The Library of Congress has cataloged the hardcover edition as follows:

Weeks, Sarah.

Two eggs, please. / Sarah Weeks ; illustrated by Betsy Lewin.—1st ed.

p. cm.

Summary: A look at the many different ways to prepare the very same food,
as everyone in a diner orders eggs.

ISBN-13: 978-0-689-83196-6 (hc)

ISBN-10: 0-689-83196-X (hc)

[1. Eggs—Fiction. 2. Diners (Restaurants)—Fiction.] I. Lewin, Betsy, ill. II. Title.

PZ7.W42215 TW 2003

[Fic]—dc21 2002005291

ISBN-13: 978-1-4169-2714-3 (pbk)

ISBN-10: 1-4169-2714-X (pbk)